BEST FRIEND'S FILTHY DILF

Straight to Gay First Time MM

Michael Levi

CONTENTS

CHAPTER 1

What was happening was something I would never forget. I would never forget it because this was all happening thanks to the fact that I couldn't control something sprouting up in me. I didn't want to admit it, but my cock was getting so hard under my shorts.

We were in the locker room. This guy was standing across from me, no more than a couple of feet. He was giving instructions to everyone. He wasn't paying attention to me, and yet I still found myself doing this, paralyzed in the spot where I found myself, wondering if…

Actually, I was doing so much more than just wondering.

I was thinking and obsessing over how he looked without his uniform on. His name… oh gosh. His name. I couldn't stop thinking about it. Something about it made me think that I wasn't really straight. I was, goddammit, and nobody would ever change that. Not even the smoking hot, perfect, attention-drawing man that was only holding the football ball in his hands.

Why was I feeling like my cock was giving somersaults in my pants?

It was pretty obvious. I was actually looking at the girl standing behind the double door in the other room. At least, that was what I was telling myself, even though it wasn't so easy. There were so many students in front of me and they were all paying attention to him, though I didn't think that any of them were actually thinking the same things I was.

I was the only one that was showings signs of being gay. And, goddammit, I wasn't and nobody would ever be able to tell me otherwise. It didn't matter how many experiences I had in the past where I experimented with other guys. Nothing of that mattered. What mattered was that I was looking for a girlfriend… and I was still a virgin.

Most of all, I was hoping, right now, that my best friend would never find out about these feelings that were sprouting up in my mind. After all, the man that was giving everyone instructions wasn't just our teacher – he was also his father! If he ever found out that I was looking at his old man as anything more than someone I knew, I was certain that he would do so much more than just kick me out of his life.

He would beat the shit out of me, I told myself.

"Hey man, you okay?" My friend asked after putting his hand on my shoulder, making me jump. Oh, shit. I didn't mean for that to happen at all. I was now certain that my friend knew something was up with me.

And yet, he was still only smiling. It didn't look like he was thinking I was thinking something I shouldn't.

"Yeah, I'm fine. I was just worried about something."

"Well, do you want to tell me what that is?" He asked, squinting slightly. His smile didn't fade, making me feel even more terrible about this. The fact that I was straight should be playing a bigger role in how I was feeling right now. After all, given that I was straight, I should not, under any circumstances, be feeling like I could imagine how his old man looked without his uniform on.

"Not right now. Maybe another time," I said and I hoped that my words were going to be enough to quench his curiosity. That was my hope because I didn't want him poking around a little more than he should, trying to find out what it was that was making me feel so worried.

"Okay. Then, I'm just going to pretend that everything is really okay with you," he said, returning his attention to his old man. I couldn't help but wonder if he wasn't thinking that this was weird. I mean, he was a student here in this college and one of the teachers was his old man.

I shook my head, deciding not to think about that much – at least, not much more than this.

"Hey, Thomas, catch," I heard someone saying. Someone? It was more like that was Mark's voice. He shot the ball toward me, just like that. He was holding it in his hands before, but now he decided to shoot me the ball without as much as giving me a warning. It happened so fast that it was like a blur. In a moment, the ball hit my face and I felt like a fool.

Especially because everyone in the locker room was laughing at me right now.

"Oh, that was so funny," someone said from the crowd, doing nothing to show how funny he found this. Ha, ha, ha. I was laughing, too. I just didn't want to show it to anyone. I wasn't going to. And I wasn't going to let anyone think that Mark had caught me off guard.

"You should be paying more attention to what's right in front of you, Thomas," the instructor said without trying to hide it. He didn't feel ashamed that he hit me with the ball like that. I was his student, goddammit! Why the hell didn't he warn me that he was going to throw the ball at me? I didn't know, but I feel infuriated and kind of betrayed. I didn't want to admit this, but I was kind of looking at Mark as someone I should look up to, someone that would be kind of a role model to me, but now…

Now he made me feel like crying, though of course, I wasn't going to do that in front of everyone. They would record me, I was sure of it.

And Mark didn't feel at all concerned by the reaction he was seeing. He didn't feel bad about me at all. He was actually laughing with everyone at me and that made me feel so much more furious at him than I was.

But this wasn't the first time that something like this was happening. I was going to get over it, I promised myself.

CHAPTER 2

It was the hour after the football practice we had. Everyone had already left the locker room. Everyone bar Mark, who was now standing across from me in the aisle between the lockers. He was in front of his locker, opening the door.

What was unusual about this? It was the fact that he was naked. Well, not fully naked, but still enough to make my dick hard even though I kept telling myself, over and over again, that I was straight. Perhaps, by hammering that into my mind, I would finally make it understand something so simple, but that wasn't exactly what was happening right now.

What was happening right now was that my body was rigid, frozen in place, just like it had been when Mark was giving instructions about the football practice.

My eyes couldn't stop dancing, scrutinizing every part of his body. His muscles, his nose, his lips, and even the bulge in his pair of boxer briefs. He wasn't ashamed of the fact that I could see everything, or maybe he was just completely immersed in what his mind was thinking, incapable of being aware of his surroundings.

My eyes didn't stop before noticing the twinkle of something on his finger. *On his marriage finger*, I corrected myself. He was married, because of course he was. Someone of his 'caliber' had to be married to a beautiful woman. It wasn't a mystery.

So, that was one more reason why I should stop whatever was happening here. I wasn't going to get laid with him - and that would be ridiculous, anyway. I would never be able to live with myself if that ever happened. I would never give in to my temptations no matter what.

I knew what the repercussions of that would be if John ever found out anything about it.

Gosh, his bulge was just so big. One of the biggest I had seen in my life and I'd seen plenty, considering all the porn movies on my computer and on my phone. I downloaded everything. Always, of course.

He closed the door, putting on his shirt and then his pair of jeans. He was getting ready to leave the campus, I told myself. He was probably going home to see his wife and then they would even kiss before making love.

My eyes went down one more time, finding his bulge. After taking his shower – and I made sure that we didn't take shower at the same time – he turned around, seeing me.

His eyes widened slightly. I had already finished putting on my clothes. I had to because the last thing I wanted was Mark possibly noticing my boner. Gosh, if that had happened, I would have fainted.

"Thomas, I didn't know that you were still here," he said, approaching me. He was coming over to me, I thought while feeling like fainting. But I wasn't going to. It didn't matter that his presence was overwhelming – he wasn't going to make me faint.

Not to mention that John would find out about it, so it really couldn't happen at all.

"Yeah, I was just getting some of my stuff. You know, there's so much to study when I get home, so I want to make sure I'm not leaving anything behind," I said, rubbing the back of my head. Goddammit. I shouldn't have done that. I should also not have smiled nervously because I was certain that he had noticed it. He was pretty smart and he knew something was up with me.

"You are in Civil Engineering, right?" He asked, putting his arm on the locker by my side. As he did that, my eyes scrutinized the way that his muscles moved and bulged. I swear it was like he was a god.

"Yeah, I am," I replied, fading my smile. Good, I thought. I wasn't suddenly going to ruin everything that was going well for me in my life because I had a crush on my teacher – a crush that I couldn't understand well, anyway.

"It's probably pretty hard, isn't it?" He asked, continuing the small talk he was making with me. I couldn't believe that we were making small talk in the locker room.

Was he studying me? I didn't know, but the more time continued to pass, the more I thought that just might be the case.

"Yeah, it's pretty hard. I always have to study so much."

"Well, I'm no expert in math and physics, but if you need help, I could help you. I know some things that might help you with your homework," he offered, his eyes remaining serious about this. He was actually offering to help me with my homework? I should be thankful for that, but the only thing I could actually keep thinking about was what would happen if we were alone in my house or… in his.

Would he ever do it with a man? I didn't know. All I knew was that him standing so close to me was making me realize that I could feel the smell of his body. It was tantalizing. It was tempting. Mark was so much more masculine than me, especially thanks to that chest hair poking out of the collar of his shirt.

Gosh, I was beginning to admit to myself that I might not be as straight as I thought I was.

"Well, I'm going to keep that in mind," I said, whirling around and then getting my things. My mind was such a mess of different thoughts I didn't even realize that I had forgotten my notebook behind. So, I turned back around straight away and picked it up in a blur with my hand.

Mark didn't say anything as I left the locker room. I thought that he was at least going to say goodbye to me, but he didn't. He actually stayed in the locker room, most likely wondering what it was that could be wrong with me right now.

And I was certain that he was going to find out I was gay… Or at least bi.

CHAPTER 3

It was another day after the football training and again I found myself in the locker room and alone with the coach. Just like last time, he was naked, and this time I was making sure that I wasn't making it too obvious that I was looking. I still stole a few glances whenever I could, though.

What was I thinking was going to happen after this? I didn't know. I was taking my time putting on my clothes because I wanted to be stealing glances at his mesmerizing body. I had wondered before so many times how he looked without his uniform on, and now I could see it again, just like that other day when I thought he was going to find out I had a crush on him.

Mark closed the door of the locker. I put everything I brought here into my backpack, and I was turning around in a heartbeat, hoping that he wasn't going to notice that I was still here. He had his earphones on and was talking with someone, who was most likely his wife.

Gosh, why was it that my mind could not understand he was off-limits? I asked myself, hating that these feelings were showing all of a sudden again. Forget the part about being 100% straight. That couldn't be any further from the truth.

And I was really going to leave the locker room, but then I heard his voice. He called out to me. Mark asked me to stop and I had to. I would not have stopped if he was someone else, but he was Mark and he was my crush, the one making me realize that I wasn't as straight as I had thought before.

"Thomas, I have something to say to you," he said and I thought that the next thing he was going to say to me was that he knew all about what I was thinking and that he was going to tell John everything. It would be the end of our friendship.

I froze up where I was, turning around and smiling, rubbing the back of my head again. It was all happening just like on that day, I thought. It was frightening to realize that.

"Yes, Prof. Robins?" I said. I was hoping that by being so formal I was going to make my silly mind finally understand that nothing would ever come out of this, but it was still obvious that it wasn't going to give up.

"There is this party I'm going to throw at my place and I was wondering if you want to come. John is going to be there, of course, so you two will have an amazing time. No alcohol for you, as usual. You are both still under 21."

My eyes widened. The last thing I thought was going to happen was him inviting me over to his house. One more reason to think that he was planning on being alone with me in a place where nobody could see us together, like here in this locker room.

"Oh, really? That would be great," I replied. Why did I have to say that? I could have danced around the subject, making Mark give up on it. But now it was already too late.

"Yeah. You can come. I'm inviting you," he said and I felt my breath hitching in my throat. If I didn't release it, I was going to start coughing. Not to mention the reddish tint on my cheeks. I was sure that Mark was noticing it, too.

"Then, I'm definitely going," I replied and I hated myself for saying that so suddenly. I shouldn't have done it.

He settled his hand on my shoulder, squeezing the skin slightly. Gosh, my body melted again.

"I knew you were going to say that, Thomas. It's really going to be so great to have you with all of us. Oh, and we are also going to have pizza," he said like it was something I was going to be thinking about more than the fact that I was going to be in his house.

I just couldn't wrap my head around this and think that

nothing was going to come out of it.

I mean, he would never suddenly lock himself with me in his bedroom, would he?

I went back home right away and threw open the door of the bathroom, shoving down my pants. I was doing this because I wanted to jack off. I wanted to jack off because I had to do something about this suspicion that something was going to happen in Mark's house.

So, I started to pump my dick, closing my eyes and thinking about Mark and me, in his house. I imagined myself getting down on my knees and his cock standing proudly in front of me. I imagined how great it would feel, my tongue swirling around his gland, his lips murmuring over and over how great he felt with my mouth around his manhood, spurring me into thinking that it was going to lead to something more.

I knew it was crazy. I knew that it would never lead to anything, and yet I still found myself shooting my come in the toilet, panting. Wow. I just couldn't believe how fast I came. I thought that nothing in life could ever make me come so fast.

I thought that I was getting bored of the girls, thinking that they all looked alike, but that couldn't be any further from the truth. I just needed something else to get me off.

I flushed the toilet, watching the water go down with my come. Gosh, what was really going to happen when I was in Mark's house? I asked myself, turning off the light in the bathroom and then lying down on my bed, my arms spread out.

CHAPTER 4

I was at the party and it was great. Mark was here with us. He was across from me in the middle of the party, dancing with his wife. I was with some girl who was trying to hook up with me, but I wasn't interested. I wasn't interested because my eyes kept glancing to the side, always finding Mark.

Gosh, he just looked so tempting, so smoking hot. No wonder his wife married him.

"Hey, is everything okay with you?" She asked and I shook my head.

"Yeah, everything's fine. Why wouldn't it be?" I replied, destroying her attempts at prying for more information. If she was thinking that I was going to disclose something that close to me to her, then she was going to be disappointed.

"I feel like you are looking at someone or something at the party and not paying attention to me," she said, making me feel some pity for her.

"You know, I don't think that this is working," I said, moving away from her. I moved away from her and then I found myself in another spot at the party. I was hoping that here I was going to be at a place where I didn't have to be thinking about Mark as much as I was thinking right now, but I realized that that was harder to do than I'd thought. It didn't matter where I was at the party, my mind always went back to him and I always went back to thinking that perhaps he was also fantasizing about me.

At least, that was what I was thinking. Around that same

moment, when I was turning my head to look to the other side, where perhaps I could find something more interesting at the party – something for me to do – I found him. And this time, Mark was alone. I had no idea what he thought he was doing, but he was alone and he was actually staring back at me.

He was staring at me through the crowd, making me freeze right on the spot. What the hell was he thinking? Why was he staring at me? I asked myself so many times I thought that I would never stop making those questions to myself. I thought that his stare alone was going to be enough to freeze me in place so much I would never be able to leave it.

And then, he winked. He winked. What? I asked myself. Why the hell was he winking at me?

I didn't know, but that made my cock so hard. If he was winking at me – and I was assuming that right now I didn't just imagine that –it meant that something else was at play here.

Where was his wife? I asked myself.

I blinked once and he was not there anymore. I felt lost. This didn't make sense at all. He was just there no more than some seconds ago, and now he was missing. Maybe not 'missing', but I simply could not see him anywhere. And that was maddening.

I sighed and decided to go up to the second floor. I didn't want to admit this, but even though I didn't drink anything made of alcohol, I was a little tired and didn't want to go back home tonight. I didn't have to go there, anyway. I was living alone and didn't have to tell anyone about anything I did.

It was dark outside, I realized after opening my eyes and noticing that I was still in the same house. In Mark's house, I detailed. Oh, shit. The fact that I was still in his house meant that my mind was going to be thinking even harder about him than before. I was going to keep imagining that something was going to happen between us.

John was still in the house, though thankfully he was in his bedroom, so it didn't matter. At least I had my own bedroom here, I thought. There was nothing special about it, but it did give me privacy and thinking that I just couldn't stop myself before putting my fingers around my cock, stroking it.

Where was I thinking I was going with this? Obviously, I was going to come. I was going to reach my climax while thinking about Mark. It should be a reason for me to feel ashamed of myself, but that wasn't the thought that was crossing my mind at the moment.

I was thinking how much I would want to see him fully naked. I wanted to see his cock right in front of my face and him stroking it gently. But I was also aware that would never happen. He had his wife and I was certain that they had a happy life together. It would be so selfish of me to destroy it.

That was what I was telling myself, anyway, my hand shooting up and down faster, punching against my balls. I was picking up the pace. My breathing was becoming harder. I could feel a sheen of sweat covering my skin, and I could also feel that familiar sensation of pressure in my gland.

I was going to come. I was going to climax and then shoot my come all over my legs and belly. It was going to be messy, but still so good, and then I would have to take a shower to remove the smell that was going to be in the air. The last thing I wanted was anyone in this house finding out that I masturbated while I was their guest. I was certain that, if they found out about it, they would kick me out of here. I didn't want to disappoint John, either.

CHAPTER 5

But I realized that that wasn't going to be so easy. I wasn't thinking straight. My hand was still shooting up and down on my cock when I realized that it was too late. I felt my come shooting out. It was shooting up high in the air and then it fell down on my belly and my legs. I was climaxing, my breathing hard. My eyes rolled inside my head and, while this all happened, the only thing I could think about was how much I wanted to feel Mark inside of me.

Some seconds later, I regained my breathing and I could finally think better about this and I felt slightly ashamed of myself. I took one of the towels and I started to clean myself with it, removing the come that was on my body. I was naked and could feel the air in the room kissing my body.

I threw the towel into the compartment to throw towels and then I heard something weird coming from outside the house. It felt like there was someone in the swimming pool. Someone was swimming at night? I wondered, going over to the window and then looking outside, though while hiding my body as much as I could so that nobody could see that I was naked.

Then, I did find someone swimming in the swimming pool. It was a man, and the shape of his body was clear enough. The man that was swimming in the swimming pool was none other than Mark himself, and… Gosh, I just couldn't believe that one of my dreams was finally happening. He was naked. He didn't even have any underwear on. He was in the water, his arms propelling him forward efficiently.

And his body, even though it was dark outside, I could tell how perfect it was. I could tell that. It showed that he was older than me, but that he still had everything. He could dominate me so easily with such a perfect body, and I could just imagine his dominant hands flowing over my body, monopolizing me.

Just thinking about that, my cock was hard already.

I had to be going mad. I shouldn't be doing this. I was in the swimming pool with him, and he was helping me to learn how to swim. He told me that one of the things I should learn now that I was an adult was how to swim, and well, me being me, I just couldn't refuse the offer. So, he was behind me and with his hands supporting my weight, pushing me up so that I didn't fall deeper into the water. The best thing about this? It was that I was getting comfortable with the idea of letting him fuck me.

At least, that was what I was telling myself.

"Yeah, just like this. This is how you can float on the water," he murmured, and I noticed that his mouth was so close to my ear that I could just imagine his lips kissing me. But the problem with that was that I knew he would never. After all, he still had his marriage ring on his finger and his wife was in the house.

I just couldn't help but wonder if this was something he did often.

"This is the first time that you are skinny dipping?" I then finally asked, and he chuckled.

"It's not the first time, but what's the first time about this is that I'm actually helping someone learn how to swim. John, even though he's my son, doesn't really get along with me. He would never let me teach him how to swim, so this is something that I'm doing with you and it's really fulfilling. It's like I'm finally doing something I skipped in my entire life."

So here I was bonding with Mark and I just couldn't wrap my head around it. It was happening so sweetly, so quickly, and we were both naked. He wasn't ashamed that he was seeing my nakedness. It was all jaw-dropping, really.

I closed my eyes and while I thought about nothing in particular that didn't involve feeling his hands touching my skin, I gasped when I felt his fingers going around my cock.

For a moment, I didn't know what was happening, and then I reopened my eyes and I found his eyes looking back at me. Mark was smiling softly, and I knew he had something he wanted to say to me.

"You like it when I do this, don't you?" He asked, murmuring. His voice was nothing but a whisper, but I could still hear his words as if he was speaking normally to me.

I was nervous and yet I wasn't going to lie to him, especially when his eyes were studying me so carefully. He was examining my facial reactions and I knew that he would know the truth if I lied. So, no matter what happened, I wasn't going to lie to him.

I nodded and he widened his smile slightly. His hand continued to stroke my cock gently, focusing on the other side of the gland.

"And I really like doing this, too. Your cock isn't so big, but there's still something special about it. You know, I've never told this to anyone, but I've always been bi, so I feel like I'm doing one more thing I thought I would never do in my life."

Was I hearing this right? Was he really telling me that he was into me and that he wanted to have sex with me? I just couldn't believe it, but I was still going on with this. My balls were hot and my cock was rock hard, and whatever was going to happen from now on, it couldn't be stopped.

"And, here, I'm going to do this. You really want me to do this with you, don't you?" He asked while looking into my eyes. To be honest, it would have been difficult to say no even if I wanted to.

I nodded and then he helped me stay in the water so that I was still floating in it but my body was 'standing'. Then, he went into the water and grabbed my legs with his hands, positioning his head right in front of my cock.

Oh shit, was this really going to happen? Was my teacher

going to suck me off?

He put my cock into his mouth, swirling his tongue around it. I felt his fingers moving over my legs and feeling the softness of my skin. It was the first time that someone was sucking me off, so I was making sure I was making the most out of this.

And his mouth was so hot, too. His lips worked my gland with mastery, bringing me more pleasure than ever before. John could never find out about this, I thought, remembering that he was sleeping in his bedroom. Any moment now, he could look outside and find us doing this. I couldn't help but wonder what he would think.

Well, I knew what he would think, but I still wondered how all the events would play out.

I gasped when he took me deeper into his mouth, his hand working my balls and focusing on them, making me feel unforgettable things. My eyes rolled inside my head the next moment when I finally climaxed in the water and in his mouth.

He pulled himself back up and then shook his head, water drops shooting away from his hair. He swallowed all of my come and that was unbelievable. I was looking at him now while showing that was exactly what I was thinking, and he was smiling, showing me that he couldn't care less.

"Your come is really nice. Salty. Hot. I love it. I want more, but I think that a virgin like you is probably looking for something else too, isn't that right?" He asked, turning me around and then positioning himself behind me. His finger found my butthole and he started to work on it, making me moan and groan. Though, when he realized that I was making too much noise, he closed his hand on my mouth, stopping me from ruining this impossibly hot moment we were having together.

I nodded. What would be the point of lying right now, anyway? There was no point in doing that, so I accepted his offer right away, and some minutes later, when he thought that he loosened up my asshole a little more, he plunged his dick right inside of me, and... wow. I felt like he was everywhere inside of me, pushing against my prostate, and then he started to piston in and out of me, finally taking my virginity.

And the best thing about this? It was the fact that I could imagine moments like this one happening so many times in the future, his dick always inside of me. He was cheating on his wife with me, and that thought alone, instead of making me feel ashamed of myself, made me feel the opposite.

"You are so tight, Thomas," he murmured, jamming his prick all the way inside of me and then shooting his load in my rectum, branding me as his, and this couldn't be any different.

I was making a promise to myself.

No matter what happened in the coming months, I was always going to be his little bitch, just like it was happening right now.

EPILOGUE

So, I had this friend and I was chatting with him on the phone. His name was Allen and we were really good friends. So much so that I was telling him everything about what happened. Everything that happened when I was in Mark's house.

He was flabbergasted, of course. It was the only normal reaction that anyone would have after hearing everything I just told him.

"You can't really be serious about this. You just fucked your own teacher and- and now you are in a happy relationship with him? Don't get me wrong, I know that you are telling me the truth, but it still feels like you are living in a dream."

"I know how this looks, but trust me when I say that I'm not lying about this at all. He's actually here with me. He's listening to our little chat, and he is laughing about it. He wants to see you, too. That is if you are interested."

"I'm not going anywhere! I'm straight. I mean, don't get me wrong. I'm happy that you're happy with him, but I just don't want to see myself embroiled in something so dramatic as what is happening in your life. I mean, so many things could go wrong. His wife could finally find out the whole truth, and I'm certain that she would do so much more than just yell at you."

I chuckled. "You have a good point, but... Well, I've given you my invitation and I'm hoping that you think about it deeply. I want you to open your mind and accept new experiences, just like it happened with me and Mark."

"Yeah, we'll see about that." And after he said that, we chatted a little more and then I turned off the call, and then I returned my attention to Mark, who was with his arm around me. I could feel the weight of it. I could feel the warmth coming from his body, and the only thing I wanted to do right now was to kiss him on his lips. We were in his house. I came here after he told me that his wife had traveled somewhere far away from the country, so this was the opportunity we wanted to have so that we could experience so much more.

I didn't stop myself before sneaking my hand under his pants, putting my fingers around his monstrous cock. It was so big that my hand felt tiny in comparison, and yet I still didn't stop myself before lowering his pants and putting his dick into my mouth, which was exactly how I wanted to kickstart this afternoon.

After all, it was still summer, and it was so hot that the only thing I wanted to do with him was to go skinny dipping together in his swimming pool again.

Just like during our first time.

The End

Don't forget to leave your review. It really helps me a lot :)

TEASER: BOYFRIEND'S NAUGHTY DILF

Straight to Gay First Time MM (College Experiences - 2)

"Come on, come play with me," Chuck said, making the ball bounce with him. I approached him, but I had no idea if I was going to make a fool of myself or not. The reason for that was simple. This was the first time I was playing basketball.

I'd told him that before.

We were in the court between the buildings where my boyfriend lived. It was his father who was playing basketball with me, and he made me feel something different. Something that I couldn't put my finger on.

I didn't want to think that I was creating, in my mind, sexual thoughts involving him, but sometimes that was exactly what happened, and I felt terrible about it. I felt terrible about it because I wanted to be loyal to my boyfriend, even though, sometimes, it was difficult to do so.

I just couldn't stop watching the ball bounce in front of him. His hands made the ball shoot up and down, moving in a blur. The way that he was doing that, it was obvious that he was teasing me, and… It was making this so much more difficult for me.

It was like that because I wore basketball shorts and they weren't my size. In fact, they were a size too small, which made me fear that my boyfriend was going to find out I had a boner while looking at his father. It wouldn't be so bad if my eyes weren't showing so much lust, too, I thought.

I shook my head, shooing those thoughts out of my mind. They weren't going to help me with anything.

Chuck was much bigger than me, no denying it. I took some steps toward him, and I tried to make myself look as menacing as I could, positioning my body so that I was protecting the basket behind me.

Chuck had already scored once and I couldn't let him do the same again. Not even over my dead body, I thought, also trying to make myself look like I could actually make all of that happen. He couldn't hide the chuckle that came out of his mouth, could he?

I was such a fool, behaving in this manner. He had a convincing, cocky smile on his face, and he knew that he was better than me in basketball. It wasn't even a contest, I told myself.

The sun was bright and warm today, shining on my face. It was just over the buildings, and thankfully it was behind me. The fact that it was positioned over there meant that I could see Chuck in all his glory, his body glistening under the light, looking more and more capable of making me feel even more turned on than I already was.

My mind was so dirty, and I felt horrible that I couldn't do anything about it.

"You're not going to score again!" I affirmed, but I didn't think that I was going to be able to follow through with that, not without looking like a fool, anyway.

Chuck leaped, shooting his body in my direction. He was like a lightning bolt, his body moving as if he were the wind. The ball bounced with him. His hand went up and down. In the meantime, I couldn't stop checking his body from bottom to top. He was so masculine, so virile, and also so much bigger and taller than me. In comparison to him, I was a nobody. That was something I would never tell Victor, of course.

A round of steps surrounded the basketball court. They composed the stands, and my boyfriend was the only member of the audience. He waved his hands over his head, yelling, "do your best, Robert! I know you can do it. I know that you can beat him."

I was going to try, even though my body was begging for me to do something that I shouldn't. It was begging me to touch, graze, and rub my body on Chuck's again, something I was certain was going to happen in less than a few seconds.

Why? It was pretty simple. Chuck was rushing toward me, making the ball bounce left and right, the sweat glistening on his face. He wasn't afraid of barging his body against mine, and I was certain he was going to do that without showing an ounce of remorse. That was how he was all the time, after all.

In fewer than a few seconds, he did exactly that, and he was like a speeding train blasting against me. My body fell over on the hard pavement that composed the basketball court, and even though I should be angered by that, I felt the opposite.

My erection grew bigger in an instant, something that made me feel angry at myself. I was angry at myself instead of being angry at Chuck for being such a jerk. This was basketball. Nothing more than that! That was what I told myself anyway, now feeling more like a fool than ever before.

I had already told him I wasn't a professional in basketball, and I was certain he was using that knowledge to his advantage, throwing his weight around.

And the worst thing about all this, which was also the best one? It was that it was working for him.

I heard the ball falling into the basket, and I knew that he'd just upped his advantage again, showing me once again that I couldn't compete at all. "Goddammit," I muttered, cursing to myself.

"I scored again," he said, smiling from ear to ear. It was incredible how happy he was with himself. That was one of the things about him that reminded me he was always so overconfident. He was always so cocky.

"Yeah, yeah," I grumbled, standing up. "I think that I'm tired. I don't want to play basketball anymore today," I said after looking at the sun and realizing that it was setting behind the buildings, orange tones replacing the blue ones. It was happening so quickly, the change of day to dusk, I realized.

He patted me on the shoulder and then brought his arm around my back, letting all the weight of it fall onto my body. It was quite heavy. Perhaps it was one-third of my weight, and that was me being conservative with my estimate.

"Don't worry about it, *sport*. You are going to do better after you practice a little more with me," he announced, and I looked at his face, finding out that he wasn't joking about that.

Chuck was actually planning on playing basketball with me again in the coming days, and I couldn't help but wonder if I was going to be able to survive it. After all, my boner was already beginning to show under my shorts.

I'd also just noticed that Victor was coming over, jogging. He stopped when he was with me and then Chuck removed his arm from over my shoulders, something that made me feel slightly disappointed.

I thought that he was going to walk with me all the way to his apartment while keeping his arm over my shoulders.

When his arm was pressing down on my shoulders, I could feel how hard and firm his muscles were, making me wonder how he looked without his clothes on.

All of them.

And now I was feeling even worse. I had just let that thought into my mind and it was voluntary; I didn't try to stop it while it was still time. I didn't want to be feeling and thinking that way about Chuck, even though it seemed that Victor was already noticing it, which meant that it was too late and I couldn't do anything about it anymore.

I guessed that meant we were going to have a long, accusatory argument when we were alone in Chuck's apartment.

In about a minute.

SIMILAR BOOKS

SERIES - BICURIOUS GUYS

1. Caught Looking by the Quarterback

2. Caught Looking by the Basketeer

3. Caught Looking by the Dropout

4. Caught Looking by the Jock

5. Caught Looking by the Roommate

SERIES - GAY FOR BLUE COLLARS

1. Given to the Cop

2. Given to the Miner

3. Given to the Plumber

4. Given to the Firefighter

5. Given to the Mechanic

ABOUT THE AUTHOR

Steamy MM stories, baby! Michael Levi can't go a day without sitting down and putting into words all the dirty scenes that sprout in his mind. His collection is diverse, but it's gay love only. And if you are looking for something free, check his mailing list. Warning: it can be extra spicy.

When Michael Levi isn't writing, he's chilling out by the lake close to his house. Nothing better than kicking back with a martini in his hand as he daydreams his next explicit scenes.